the CRitteR club

:paw: Liz's Night at the Museum :paw:

by Callie Barkley :heart: illustrated by Tracy Bishop

LITTLE SIMON

New York London Toronto Sydney New Delhi

LITTLE SIMON

An imprint of Simon & Schuster Children's Publishing Division · 1230 Avenue of the Americas, New York, New York 10020 · First Little Simon hardcover edition October 2016 · Copyright © 2016 by Simon & Schuster, Inc. All rights reserved, including the right of reproduction in whole or in part in any form. LITTLE SIMON is a registered trademark of Simon & Schuster, Inc., and associated colophon is a trademark of Simon & Schuster, Inc. For information about special discounts for bulk purchases, please contact Simon & Schuster Special Sales at 1-866-506-1949 or business@simonandschuster.com. The Simon & Schuster Speakers Bureau can bring authors to your live event. For more information or to book an event contact the Simon & Schuster Speakers Bureau at 1-866-248-3049 or visit our website at www.simonspeakers.com. Designed by Laura Roode · The text of this book was set in ITC Stone Informal Std. Manufactured in the United States of America 0916 MTN
10 9 8 7 6 5 4 3 2 1
Cataloging-in-Publication Data for this title is available from the Library of Congress.
ISBN 978-1-4814-7165-7 (hc)
ISBN 978-1-4814-7164-0 (pbk)
ISBN 978-1-4814-7166-4 (eBook)

Table of Contents

Chapter 1

It Was a Dark and Stormy Night

Liz Jenkins turned on her flashlight. She held it up to her chin so it illuminated just her face.

It was silent and shadowy in Liz's bedroom. Her best friends Ellie, Amy, and Marion waited for Liz to begin her story.

"It was a dark and stormy night," Liz said in a low voice.

"Uh-oh," said Amy. She pulled her sleeping bag up to her nose. "I don't like the sound of this."

Ellie giggled. "Stormy nights are always the spookiest!"

Marion yawned. "I think I've heard this one before," she said sleepily.

"Outside, lightning flashed," Liz continued. "Thunder clapped. But inside one house, four girls were having a sleepover."

"Just like us!" Ellie whispered.

Liz went on. "They were all in their sleeping bags. One of the girls had just finished telling a story. It

was a scary story about a ghost, with rattling, clattering footsteps roaming her house at night."

Now Amy's sleeping bag was covering her head. She let out a squeak from inside.

"Don't worry," Marion gently told Amy. "It's just a story."

Liz suddenly flicked off her flashlight. The bedroom went completely dark.

"All of a sudden, one of the girls gasped," Liz went on. "'What was that?' the girl cried. The others listened. They heard it too!"

Liz stomped her foot on the ground. "*Thwump—rattle. Thwump—rattle.* Rattling, clattering footsteps! Coming from the other side of the bedroom door!"

Marion sat up straight. "Shhh!" she said, suddenly wide-awake. "Did you hear that?"

Liz looked confused. "Hear what?" she replied. Then she smiled. "Oooh. Nice one, Marion. Trying to scare the storyteller."

Marion shook her head. Her eyes

were wide in alarm. "No. Listen!"

The four girls sat silently, listening.

They all heard it. *Thwump—rattle. Thwump—rattle. Thwump—rattle.* Each time it was a little louder.

"Rattling, clattering footsteps!" Liz whispered.

"Coming closer," Ellie said shakily.

Amy stayed hidden inside her sleeping bag. "Is it coming from the hallway?" she asked.

Liz flicked her flashlight back on. She aimed the beam at her bedroom door. Liz, Ellie, and Marion watched it, trying not to blink.

Thwump—rattle. Thwump—rattle.
Louder and louder, until . . .
  Silence.
  And then, slowly, Liz's doorknob turned.

Chapter 2

Who Ghosts There?

Ellie screamed.

Marion buried her head in her pillow.

Liz dropped her flashlight. It hit the floor and clicked off. She felt around in the darkness, trying to find it.

Amy couldn't see anything from inside her sleeping bag. "What?"

she called out. "What's going on?"

Suddenly, the bedroom light went on. Liz, Marion, and Ellie looked up. Amy peeked out of her sleeping bag.

Standing in the doorway was Liz's mom.

"Did I startle you?" she said gently. She was holding a tray with glasses of milk and some oatmeal cookies. "I'm sorry. I just came to see if you wanted a snack."

Mrs. Jenkins stepped into the room. With each step: *Thwump.* The glasses on the tray knocked

13

together: *Rattle.*

Thwump—rattle.
Thwump—rattle.
Thwump—rattle.

She put the tray down on Liz's dresser. Then she walked out.

The girls looked at one another. "A ghost that brings us snacks!" Ellie exclaimed.

They all burst out laughing.

"I guess we were a little jumpy," Marion said.

"*I* sure was!" Amy chimed in. "No more spooky stories for tonight. Okay?"

"Agreed!" said Liz. "We'll save them for the museum sleepover next Friday."

The girls had signed up for Night at the Museum. It was a once-a-year event at the Santa Vista Art and History Museum. At closing

time, about twenty-five kids got to
stay and do fun activities in the
museum. Best of all, they would
spend the night there!

"Did you know we were the first
ones to sign up?" Liz said proudly.

Ellie laughed. "You made sure of
that, Liz!"

Liz took an art history class at the museum every Saturday. One week, the teacher, Ms. Bunn, had passed out flyers about the event. Liz was so excited she called Ellie, Amy, and Marion as soon as she got home. They wanted to sign up too!

"And Ms. Bunn is going to be one of the chaperones!" Liz told them.

Liz gasped.

"I almost forgot!" she said. "This morning, in class, Ms. Bunn told me she stopped by The Critter Club. She went to meet Tiger."

Tiger was the name the girls had given to a shy stray cat they'd found. They had taken him to The Critter Club, the animal shelter they ran in their friend Ms. Sullivan's barn.

The girls had been trying to find Tiger a home for weeks.

"And the best part is," Liz continued, "Ms. Bunn wants to adopt him!"

The girls cheered.

"And she said she could come pick him up tomorrow morning,"

Liz said. "Can we all go meet her at The Critter Club?"

The girls nodded.

Ellie snapped her fingers. "It'll be perfect! She can ask us anything she needs to know about cats. And we can ask her all about the museum sleepover!"

"Like whether we'll get to sleep in the temple in the Egyptian Wing!" said Marion.

"Or in the planetarium

under the starry dome!" Amy said.

Liz imagined drifting off to sleep in a room filled with beautiful paintings. Would she dream about art? Would she even be able to fall asleep? *First things first*, Liz thought. *I have to get to sleep tonight so Friday will come sooner!*

A Cat Named Tiger

After breakfast on Sunday Liz's dad gave the girls a ride to The Critter Club. They had to look all over the barn for Tiger. Finally they found him hiding under a cabinet.

"Come on out, boy," Amy said sweetly.

Marion patted her lap gently.

"Here, kitty-kitty-kitty," sang Ellie.

Liz found Tiger's favorite cat toy—a fabric bird on the end of a string. She dangled it so the bird hovered just above the floor.

But Tiger did not come out.

"Hello?" came a voice from the doorway. The girls turned to see a tall woman wearing flowy pants and a head scarf. She waved. A few silver bracelets jangled on her wrist.

"Ms. Bunn!" Liz cried. She ran over. "Everyone, this is Ms. Bunn from the museum!"

Liz introduced her to Ellie, Amy, and Marion.

"Nice to meet you!" Ms. Bunn said. "And I'm so impressed by

The Critter Club. When Liz told me about little Tiger, I thought it must be a sign. I've been without a pet for years!"

Liz put her hands on her hips. "Well, this little Tiger is being *extra* shy today," she said. Liz showed Ms. Bunn where the cat was hiding.

"Usually we can get him to come out," Marion said. "But nothing is working."

Ms. Bunn opened her bag. "Maybe I can try," she said. "I brought him a little present."

Ms. Bunn took out a small foil packet. She opened it and put it down on the ground.

In a flash Tiger ran over. He pounced on the foil, sniffed, and began to lick the contents.

"Wow!" Liz cried. "What is that?"

Ms. Bunn smiled. "Tuna fish. I guess he likes it!"

Within minutes Tiger had eaten it all. He inched over to Ms. Bunn and sniffed at her jangly bracelets. Then he rubbed his head against her arm.

"I guess he likes *you*, too!" Ellie said.

The girls gathered some supplies for Ms. Bunn to take with her: cat

food, kitty litter, Tiger's cat toys.

Ms. Bunn thanked them and told them not to worry. "I've had many cats over the years," she said. "Some of them were also shy. But we understood each other."

The girls watched as the cat let Ms. Bunn pet him. He purred softly.

"Well," said Marion. "Sounds like you two are a *purr*-fect match!" She giggled.

"We've been calling him Tiger," Amy said. "But maybe *you* want to name him?"

Ms. Bunn smiled. "I *did* have a name in mind," she said. "Picasso. After Pablo Picasso, my favorite artist."

Liz gasped. "I love Picasso too!" she cried. "Ooh! Isn't there a part of the museum with

some Picasso paintings? Can we go there on Friday?"

"Where will we be sleeping?" Amy chimed in.

"And what should we bring?" Marion asked.

"What time is lights-out?" Ellie asked. "Or can we stay up all night?"

Ms. Bunn laughed. "So many questions!" she cried. "I'll try to answer them all." She sat down with Tiger-now-Picasso on her lap and began.

The Longest Day Ever

Liz's week flew by. Before she knew it, it was Thursday night and time to pack. They'd leave for the museum on Friday right after school!

Ms. Bunn had given the girls a helpful packing list. Many of the items made it sound like they were packing for camp.

Packing List
- ☐ Sleeping bag
- ☐ Pillow
- ☐ Pajamas
- ☐ Slippers
- ☐ Toothbrush
- ☐ Toothpaste
- ☐ Flashlight
- ☐ Change of clothes
- ☐ Snack

But in other ways it was different. No bug spray. No hiking shoes. No bathing suit. You didn't need much for camping indoors!

Liz checked off all the items. Her bag was just about full. She tossed in a granola bar for a snack. Then she spotted her sketch pad and colored pencils on her desk. She packed those, too.

On Friday morning Liz hurried into school. She was ready to get the school day started . . . and finished! Then they'd be off to the museum.

Liz dove into her morning work. It was a worksheet on telling time. *I wish I* could *tell time,* Liz thought. *I'd tell it to go faster!* She looked up at the clock. The hands had barely moved since she'd gotten to school!

On the spelling test, all the words had the long *e* sound.

"The next word is *sleep*," Mrs. Sienna said.

Liz wrote the word and kept on going: *sleepover*. She realized just in time and erased the last four letters.

During writing time Liz worked on her biography of Eleanor Roosevelt. Or she tried to. Twice she realized she was doodling, not writing.

Liz usually loved reading group. But she kept losing her place in her book. It was so hard to concentrate!

At lunch she sat near Ellie, Marion, and Amy. But they couldn't talk much about the sleepover. There were other kids at their table too. Liz didn't want them to feel left out.

Even art class—her favorite— seemed to drag on. She liked how her pinch pot was turning out. But it made her wish she were at the museum, looking at the ceramics collection.

Finally, after the longest hour of math ever, it was time for dismissal!

Out front, the girls spotted Liz's mom pulling up in her van. "Ready to go?" Mrs. Jenkins called out the window.

Liz slid the back door open. "I've

been ready all day!" she replied.
The girls climbed in.

Mrs. Jenkins had already stopped
by each girl's house to pick up her
things. So they headed right to the
museum.

When they were almost there,

Liz cried out, "Oh, no! I forgot Elly!"

Ellie tapped Liz on her shoulder. "Uh . . . I'm right here."

Liz laughed and shook her head. "No," she said. "I mean Elly, my stuffed elephant."

Her friends knew *that* Elly too. Liz had had her since she was three. She liked to sleep with her at night. Especially when she was away from home.

Ellie Mitchell gave Liz's hand a

squeeze. "Don't worry about it," she said.

"We'll all be together," Amy added.

"Besides," said Marion, "it's a museum. Not a haunted house."

Liz Gets Lost!

"Wow," Liz whispered to Ellie. "It's so quiet in here."

Ms. Bunn was leading the sleepover group on a museum tour. For some, it was their first time at the museum.

Liz, on the other hand, had been there lots of times. But she was used to seeing it crowded. And *hearing*

it crowded. Sure, people tried to be quiet in a museum. But lots of people trying to be quiet is still pretty loud.

Now their group was the only one in the whole museum. In the silence, every little noise seemed big. Their footsteps echoed off the marble walls. Ms. Bunn dropped her pen. It *clickety-clacked* across the shiny floor.

There were twenty other kids besides Liz and her friends. Each group of four had a chaperone. Ms. Bunn was the chaperone for Liz and her friends.

"How is Picasso doing?" Liz asked Ms. Bunn as they walked.

"Very well!" Ms. Bunn replied. "He found his favorite hiding places in my house. Under my bed. Or behind the sofa. But he always comes out for snacks."

Ms. Bunn moved quickly through the exhibits. "We'll have more time to look at things in the morning,"

she told the group. "For now, just take it all in. Think about what you want to come back to."

They walked through the sculpture garden. They moved on through Early American Quilts and into Twentieth-Century Inventors.

Then they headed into the painting galleries.

These were Liz's favorite rooms. One room was filled with water-color paintings. In the next room were oil paintings from the 1600s.

When they got to the Modern Art Wing, Liz stopped. This was

where the Picasso paintings and other abstract art were.

Some of the artwork was so simple.

Other pieces were complicated. Liz thought they weren't so much paintings of things but of feelings.

Like anger. Or joy. Or sadness.

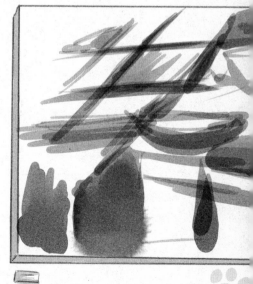

Liz looked around. Where was everyone? Suddenly, she was all alone in the gallery.

"Hello?" Liz called. Only her own voice echoed back at her.

Uh-oh, I'd better find the group! Liz thought.

Liz hurried on to the next room. There was no one there. Beyond that room, Liz had to make a choice. Go left to Rocks and Gems? Or go right to Age of Dinosaurs?

Liz thought she heard a noise from the right. So she went that way. "Hello?" she called again.

The room was dim. A few small lights shone up from beneath the T. rex skeleton. They cast long shadows onto the ceiling. Liz could see outlines of dark figures. But as her eyes adjusted, she realized they were models of dinosaurs. Not people.

T. rex

She had picked the wrong way. She turned to go back toward Rocks and Gems. Just as she did, she heard something.

A scratchy, scraping sound.

Liz whipped back around. It had definitely come from inside Age of Dinosaurs. But where? It was hard to tell. Liz scanned the room again. Everything was absolutely still.

Liz stared at the T. rex. It stared back, motionless.

Then Liz slowly backed out of the room.

Last One Awake

On the other side of Rocks and Gems, Liz found the group in the Great Hall. It was a big room right in the center of the museum. Medieval tapestries hung from the walls. The furniture was dark wood with lots of carvings. A few suits of armor stood at attention.

"Where were you?" Amy asked Liz.

"I was looking at paintings," Liz explained. "Then I took a wrong turn. And it was kind of weird. I heard a—"

"Okay! Attention, everybody!" Ms. Bunn called out.

Liz stopped talking so she could listen.

"This is where we'll be sleeping," Ms. Bunn said. "Everyone find a spot and unpack your belongings!"

As she excitedly unrolled her sleeping bag and unpacked, Liz forgot all about the mysterious noise.

Soon Ms. Bunn led everyone into the museum cafeteria for dinner. They each got to top their own personal-size pizza. And they even had tofu pepperoni as a topping choice. Liz couldn't believe it. That was her favorite!

After dinner the group got to see the 3-D space show in the planetarium. With popcorn!

Then it was time to get ready for bed. The girls changed into pajamas and brushed their teeth in the bathroom.

Back in the Great Hall, Liz got out her sketch pad and pencils. She worked on a sketch of one of the suits of armor until it was time for lights-out.

"Have your flashlights handy," called Ms. Bunn, who was standing by the light

switch. Then there was a loud *click*. The overhead lights went out. "Good night, everyone!"

"Nighty-night, you guys," Ellie whispered to her friends.

"Sweet dreams!" Marion said.

"Sleep well," Amy added.

"If I can sleep at all," Liz said.

"This is just *so* cool."

Liz lay there for a while with her eyes wide open. She listened to the silence all around her. The big museum silence.

Now and then someone would cough. Or roll over in their sleeping bag. But soon all Liz could hear was breathing and quiet snores.

It was the sound of everyone asleep—except her.

Liz closed her eyes. She counted backward from one hundred. It was her best trick for falling asleep.

Liz was only at ninety when she heard something. Her eyes popped open.

What was that?

It sounded like . . . something fluttering. Or maybe it was flapping?

And just as suddenly, it stopped.

Liz sat up and looked around. Small lights lit up the corners of the room. But most of the hall was dark and shadowy. Liz looked at the suit of armor closest to her. If she didn't know better, she might have guessed it was a real person.

Liz was about to lie down again when the knight's helmet *moved*!

Liz blinked her eyes hard. *It couldn't have.* She sat staring at it for a full minute. But it was absolutely still. *You're being so silly!* she told herself.

Liz lay down and pulled her sleeping bag up to her nose. She really wished she hadn't left Elly at home.

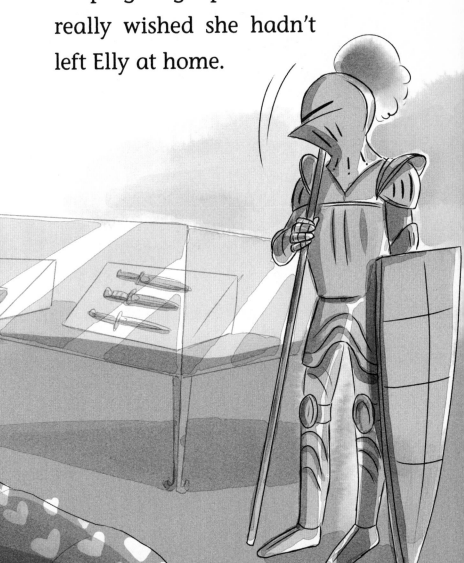

Chapter 7

Things That
Go Flap in the Night

Liz started counting backward again. She got all the way to zero and started over.

Then she heard that same noise. *Flap-flap-flap-flap-flap!*

Liz opened her eyes. Just then, she thought she saw a shadow swoop overhead. But she blinked and it was gone.

Liz leaned over toward Ellie. "Did you hear that?" she whispered.

Ellie rolled over and kept on sleeping.

"*Psst*. Ellie?" Liz whispered. She felt bad about waking up her friend. But she also didn't like being the only one awake!

Liz gave Ellie a little poke on the shoulder. "Did you hear that?"

Ellie opened one eye. "Hear what?" she mumbled.

"Listen," Liz whispered. "There's a weird noise."

Marion rolled over and opened her eyes. "What weird noise?" she whispered. She propped herself up on her elbows.

"Shhh," whispered Liz. "Just listen for a second."

"What's the matter?" whispered Amy. Her eyes were still closed.

"Liz says there's a noise," Marion said. "I only hear the noise of us talking about the noise. How about we go back to sleep?"

"But I definitely *heard* something," said Liz. "And I think I *saw* something too." Liz paused. "I . . . I think I saw the knight *move*."

"What?" said Amy.

"And a shadow flying over us!"
Liz added.

Ellie patted Liz on the back. "I
think you're just tired," Ellie said.
"Maybe you did hear something.
But I'm sure it's just some boring
old noise museums make at night.
Not a haunted-knight noise."

At that moment the noise echoed through the hall. *Flap-flap-flap-flap-flap!* It was softer than before, but clear as day.

Ellie sat up straight. "Ohmygosh, ohmygosh!" she whispered frantically. "It's a haunted-knight noise for sure!"

"Yeah, I heard that too," Amy whispered, suddenly wide-awake.

"Same," said Marion. She flicked on her flashlight. "It sounded like it was coming from over there." She aimed her flashlight toward the entrance of Rocks and Gems.

Liz pulled out her flashlight too.

"Well, I don't think I can sleep. Not until I figure out what it is."

"Let's go find out!" Ellie whispered excitedly. She clicked on her flashlight.

Finally, Amy turned hers on. "I'm not staying here alone," she said. "Plus, this sort of feels like a Nancy Drew mystery."

The four girls tiptoed across the hall. They stopped at the entrance to Rocks and Gems.

ROCKS
AND
GEMS

Liz clutched Ellie's arm. Marion and Amy linked elbows. They aimed their flashlights all around the big room. Gemstones sparkled as the beams of light moved across them.

Flap-flap-flap-flap-flap! There was the noise again. The girls' heads turned in the same direction.

"It's coming from the dinosaur rooms!" said Liz.

They tiptoed quickly in that direction, listening for the sound again. They got to the rooms with the dinosaurs and stopped.

To Liz, the room looked even spookier than before. The dim lighting. The shadows. The T. rex skeleton that seemed to be staring right at them. Liz felt Ellie squeeze her arm. Liz squeezed hers back.

The girls stood there frozen, waiting for something to happen. Waiting to hear the noise again.

Flap-flap-flappety-flap! Scritch-scratch, rustle, rustle.

They all jumped. It was different this time. And louder—closer!—than ever.

In fact, it seemed to be coming from the T. rex!

T. rex

Chapter 8

Unexpected Visitors

Scritch-scratch, rustle, rustle.
Scritch-scratch, rustle.

The girls stared at one another, trying to figure out what they were hearing.

"Wait a second," Liz whispered. "I don't think it's coming from the T. rex. It's coming from *behind* it."

The girls inched forward. They

walked a wide circle around the skeleton. As they did, their flashlights lit up the room.

The girls stopped.

There—under the T. rex's tail— were two birds.

The girls' eyes met. They all breathed a sigh of relief.

"Awwwww," Liz cooed. "They must have been in the Great Hall before. And that's what I saw fly away from the knight."

Amy leaned in to get a better look at them. Startled, the birds took flight.

Flap-flap-flap-flap-flap! They landed a few yards away on a museum sign.

"I wonder how they got in," Amy said. "Poor little guys. They can't find their way out."

Ellie inched closer to the birds. "Oh, I bet they're missing their friends!"

The birds flew away again. This time they landed way up high on the head of a pterodactyl model.

"Come on, birdies," Ellie called to the birds. "Wanna go out? Do ya?"

Liz smiled. Ellie sounded like she was talking to her dog, Sam. But unlike Sam, the birds didn't come running.

"If we could get them to follow us," Liz said, "we could *lead* them to a way out."

"But they're too afraid," Marion said.

Hmm, thought Liz. How could they get the birds to come down?

Suddenly, she exclaimed, "I've got it! Tiger—I mean Picasso—and the tuna fish!"

Ellie, Amy, and Marion looked

93

confused. "Huh?" said Amy.

But Liz was already hurrying out of Age of Dinosaurs. "Be right back!" she told them.

Liz ran on tiptoe back to the Great Hall. She went to her bag and took out the granola bar. Then she ran back to the girls. The birds were still up on the pterodactyl's head.

"What are you doing?" Marion asked.

Liz unwrapped the bar. She broke off two small pieces and put them on the floor. Then she took a few steps back.

"Aha," said Amy. "Lure them with food! Like Ms. Bunn lured Tiger out with the tuna fish!"

Liz nodded. She held up the granola bar. "It's got sunflower seeds in it!" Liz said. "They should like it. Right?"

The girls shrugged. "We'll find out soon enough," said Marion.

Chapter 9

The Escape Route

The girls stood still, watching and waiting from a distance.

Within moments one of the birds came flying down. It landed next to a granola piece. It looked over at the girls.

Then it started pecking at the granola.

The other bird flew down too. It

pecked at the other piece.

The girls cheered silently. It worked!

"Quick!" said Amy. "Let's put down more pieces over here." She hurried to the exit of the room.

"Yeah!" said Ellie. "We can make a trail of crumbs. And lead them to a way out!"

Liz put down two more pieces. The girls backed away.

The birds flew to the crumbs. *Peck-peck-peck.*

The girls kept going. Liz put down two more pieces and backed away.

The birds flew over again. *Peck-peck-peck.*

"Where are we leading them?" Marion asked. "Liz, how much granola bar is left?"

Liz looked down at the bar. "Less than half," Liz replied. "We need the shortest way out of here."

"Like a window," Ellie said.

The girls looked around. They were now in Rocks and Gems. This room didn't have any windows. Liz thought she remembered seeing one . . . but where? When she was brushing her teeth?

"The bathroom!" Liz exclaimed. "I think there was a window in there."

The bathrooms were right between Rocks and Gems and the Great Hall. Liz put down granola pieces leading to the bathroom door. The birds followed.

The girls backed into the bathroom. Yes! There *was* a small window high up on one wall. Liz carefully climbed up and onto the sink counter to slide it open.

She put two pieces of the granola bar on the windowsill. She also reached outside to put the last two crumbs on the ledge.

Meanwhile, Amy was holding

the bathroom door open, hiding behind it so the birds couldn't see her.

Liz got down from the window. She, Ellie, and Marion backed away.

Sure enough, the birds waddled into the bathroom. They flew up to the windowsill and ate the granola.

They hopped onto the window ledge. *Peck-peck-peck.*

Then they looked around. They seemed to realize they were out in the fresh air. They spread their wings.

Flap-flap-flap-flap!

And they were gone!

Chapter 10

The Haunted Museum

Liz woke up to a warm ray of sunlight on her face. Sun streamed in through the skylight of the Great Hall.

Liz sat up and stretched. Marion, Amy, and Ellie were stirring too. Ellie opened her eyes and smiled at Liz.

"Did we really rescue two birds

last night?" Liz whispered. "Or did I dream that?"

Ellie grinned. "If you dreamed it, then we had the same dream."

"Good morning, everyone!" Ms. Bunn called out gently. "Time to get up, get dressed, and pack our things."

Ms. Bunn explained that the museum would open to the public at eleven a.m. Until then they had the place to themselves.

Everyone got dressed. They packed up and left their things in the museum offices. Then they went to the cafeteria for breakfast. While they ate, they took a vote on which exhibits they wanted to spend more time in.

Liz voted for Modern Art. Others voted for Space Exploration or Ancient Greece. But

Age of Dinosaurs got the most votes. So Ms. Bunn took them there first.

As they went Ms. Bunn talked a little about the museum's history.

"It was built in 1929," she said. "It started small. At first all it held was the art collection of one wealthy Santa Vista family. Then, over the

years, it grew into what it is today. It has changed a lot since 1929."

Ms. Bunn paused. "But one thing hasn't changed," she said. "Ever since the museum was built, some have said it is haunted. There are stories of strange noises in the

Great Hall and other places. But I've worked here for years. I've never heard a thing." Ms. Bunn laughed. "Silly, right? I think ghost stories *are* just stories."

Liz, Ellie, Amy, and Marion exchanged wide-eyed looks.

"I'm glad she didn't mention that last night," Amy whispered.

"I know!" Ellie replied. "I *never* would have fallen asleep."

But Liz's mind was racing as they got to Age of Dinosaurs. She'd figured that all those noises were made by the birds. But what if they weren't?

Could some of them have been from the museum ghost?

Liz stared up at the T. rex and sighed. *He might have some stories to tell*, Liz thought. *If only extinct dinosaurs could talk!*

Read on for a sneak peek at
the next Critter Club book:

#16

Marion and the
Secret Letter

"Good morning, Teddy!" Marion said, rolling out of bed the next morning.

She went over to her dresser. She peered inside the hamster's cage.

"Where are you hiding, Teddy?" Marion said playfully. "In the tunnel again?"

But the tunnel was empty. Marion peered at the cage from all sides.

"Teddy?" Marion said, growing worried.

Gabby shuffled in, still in her pajamas. "What is it?"

"Did you take Teddy?" Marion asked, starting to panic.

"No," Gabby replied. She looked confused. "Why?"

"Teddy got out!" cried Marion. Now she was panicking. "He could be anywhere! We don't even know how long he's been out."

Before long, Marion's family had organized a search party.

Marion looked inside her closet.

There were so many places for a hamster to hide! She looked everywhere, from the top shelf to the shoe rack on the floor. They spent as long as they could searching. But no luck.

At school later Marion kept her eyes on the floor as she headed to her locker. She hoped no one asked her about Teddy. What would she say? All she wanted was to get through the day. Then she could go home and keep looking for him.

Marion opened her locker. A folded piece of paper fluttered out and landed at her feet.

If you like The Critter Club, you'll love

the adventures of
SOPHiE MOUSE

the adventures of 1
SOPHiE MOUSE
A New Friend

by Poppy Green • illustrated by Jennifer A. Bell

the adventures of 2
SOPHiE MOUSE
The Emerald Berries

by Poppy Green • illustrated by Jennifer A. Bell

the adventures of 3
SOPHiE MOUSE
Forget-me-not Lake

by Poppy Green • illustrated by Jennifer A. Bell

the adventures of 4
SOPHiE MOUSE
Looking for Winston

by Poppy Green • illustrated by Jennifer A. Bell

the adventures of 5
SOPHiE MOUSE
The Maple Festival

by Poppy Green • illustrated by Jennifer A. Bell

the adventures of 6
SOPHiE MOUSE
Winter's No Time to Sleep!

by Poppy Green • illustrated by Jennifer A. Bell

the adventures of 7
SOPHiE MOUSE
The Clover Curse

by Poppy Green • illustrated by Jennifer A. Bell

the adventures of 8
SOPHiE MOUSE
A Surprise Visitor

by Poppy Green • illustrated by Jennifer A. Bell

the adventures of 9
SOPHiE MOUSE
The Great Big Paw Print

by Poppy Green • illustrated by Jennifer A. Bell